"Sofa Boy"

Written By
Scott J. Langteau

With Illustrations By
Rion Vernon

"Sofa Boy"
Published by Shake the Moon Books.

www.shakethemoonbooks.com

ISBN - 978-0-615-25125-7.

For Dominic.

The most peculiar of events
has taken place just up the block.
Where an average little family
has sent their neighbors into shock!

It seems their quiet little boy
(you know, the one who has the slouch?)
has become lodged—if you will,
or more "at one" with his couch.

You see, he'd sit and sit and sit
on his couch the whole day through.
He'd sit intensely playing games
'til his trigger thumb turned blue!

He'd been warned that if he stayed there—
a constant blob in just one spot,
he might at some point take root.
Like a plant would, in a pot!

But while his mother shrieked in protest
reciting house-rules word for word,
he just lay there oddly trance-like.
Not a word she screamed was heard!

He heeded not her words of caution—
threw his care up to the wind,
and after months of reclining,
found himself securely pinned.

A stringy ooze had claimed the armrest
as that filthy couch took hold.
And the smell was just horrendous!
Like rotten eggs—so I've been told.

His arms and legs were soon devoured
by cushion squares and lazy glue.
And while wriggling and writhing
he dropped his best controller too!

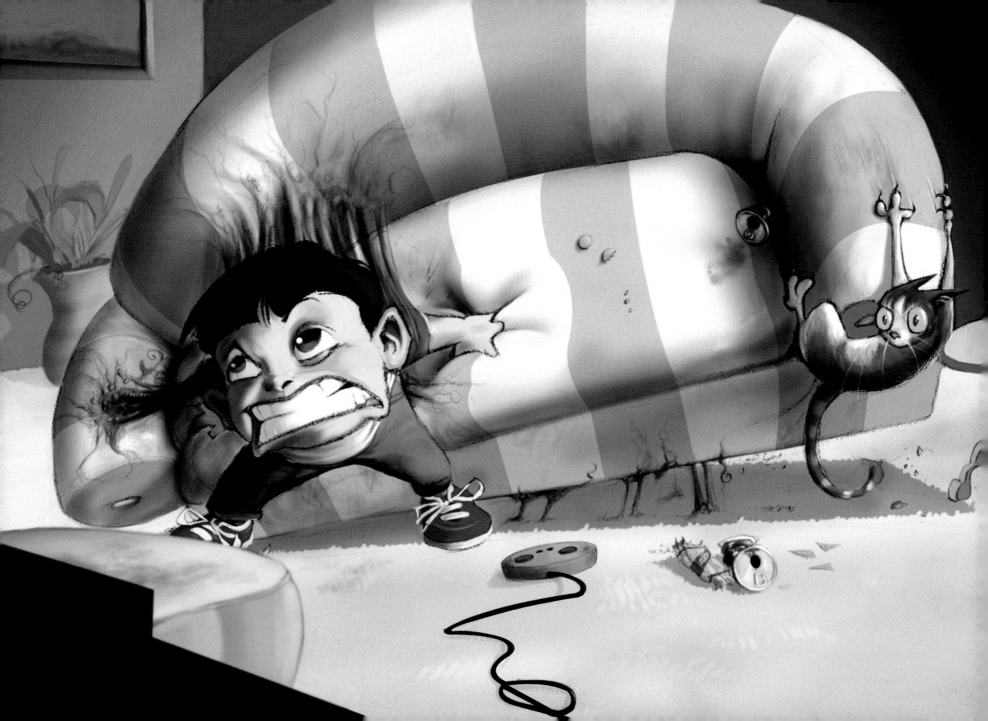

He toppled back in disbelief,
recalling all his mother said.
Only to find his hair had rooted
to the backrest beneath his head!

And then his foot just disappeared
within the footstool's goopy "grack".
It had been captured by the enemy
and would NOT be given back!

But as if that were not enough,
his cat was sealed beneath his knee.
For they'd spent their days together,
equally lazy—don't you see?

And soon the days rolled on and on
at a silent, snail-like rate,
and he grumpily surrendered
to his gruesome twist of fate.

His mother took care to tend him.
Trimmed and pruned him once a day.
While he lay there bound and rooted,
shooting dirty looks her way.

Though at last he'd learned his lesson,
wished to rise and have some fun,
his binding union with the sofa
was too far gone to be undone!

So today he's on exhibit
in the museum—it's open now.
And some say if you lean in closely...

SOFA BOY

COUCH POTATOUS CRUSTATIOUS
THIS PRIME EXAMPLE OF WHAT
HAPPENS WHEN YOU WATCH TOO
MUCH TV IS ON DISPLAY FOR ALL
TO SEE.

SCOTT

...you can still hear his cat meow!

The End.

Growing up in the small town of Seymour Wisconsin, playtime came ready-made with Scott's 11 brothers and sisters. No lie! Having fun then meant grabbing a sibling, heading outside and imagining a world around you.

That imagination brought Scott a Masters in Theater from Villanova University and to Los Angeles where he has worked as an actor, writer, and producer for nearly fifteen years. Best known for his work on the acclaimed "Medal of Honor" game franchise, Scott has worked for the likes of DreamWorks, Electronic Arts, and the Jim Henson Company.

Currently co-founder of the videogame development studio Spark Unlimited, Scott resides happily in a humble abode in North Hollywood, CA. He hopes this book (for reading!) is some small consolation for the game addictions he may have inadvertently helped inflict on so many for so long...

Scott J. Langteau

Rion Vernon

Rion Vernon, the son of an artist / designer, has been doing freelance artwork since the age of eight years old.

After graduating high school, he was hired at Stan Winston Studio (Terminator, Jurassic Park) and has continued working as a character designer for such companies as DreamWorks, Electronic Arts, Sony, Nickelodeon, Paramount and New Line Cinema.

Rion lives in Southern California working as a freelance artist. He also enjoys writing brief autobiographies in the third person.

For more information, visit:
www.shakethemoonbooks.com

SHAKE the MOON BOOKS